with ♡

The Calico Cat

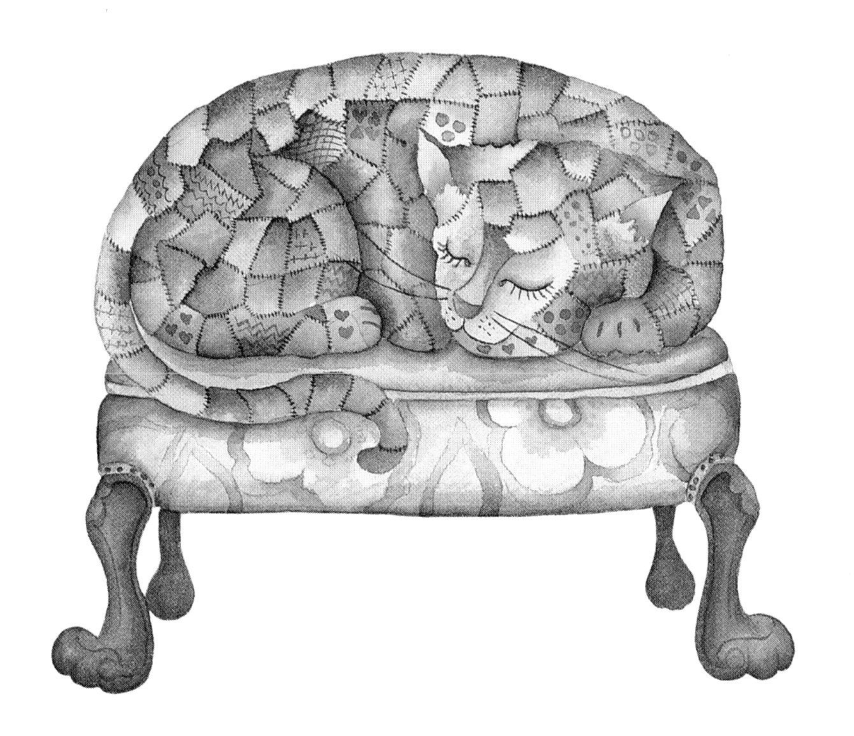

POETRY AND PAINTINGS

BY

JESSEL MILLER

The Calico Cat

ISBN: 0-9660381-8-5
Library of Congress Number: 99-095254

10 9 8 7 6 5 4 3 2 1
Editing by Carolynne Gamble
Typography & design by Jim Scott
Printed by Tien Wah Press, Singapore

Publisher's Cataloging-in-Publication
(Provided by Quality Books)

The Calico Cat / poetry and paintings by Jessel Miller. – 1st ed.
p. cm.
LCCN: 99-095254
ISBN: 0-9660381-8-5
SUMMARY: The Calico Cat changes color with her environment, and rather than go against the grain of life's experiences, chooses to blend and enjoy the changes.

1. Cats–Juvenile fiction. 2. Change (Psychology)–Juvenile fiction. 3. Protective coloration–Juvenile fiction. 4. Color of animals –Juvenile fiction. I. Title.

PZ8.3.M616Ca 1999 [E]
QBI99-884

The Calico Cat

Dedication

This book is dedicated to
all the children of the world
and
all the creatures
great
and
small.

May their lives be filled
with the
simple pleasures
this sweet cat
enjoys.

When Calico Cat was just a kitten

Barely the size of a child's mitten,

Her mother would preen her and

Clean her and wean her,

And kitty would smile

Feeling loved all the while.

DAD

She found that she grew
Each day she looked anew,
Her thoughts would be changing
Her coat rearranging,
Constantly matching the view.

Each day when she would play
Her heart would be so gay,
Her outlook was rosy
From her head to her toesy
In oh such a loveable way.

JACK
A
B
C

And when she would tire of flitting
Of running and jumping and spitting,
She'd lie on her bed
And get lost in her spread
She thought she was most befitting.

Home Sweet Home
MOM

And when it was raining
Instead of complaining,
The Calico Cat would go walking
And singing and talking
To all of the flowers for hours and hours.

CALICO
CAT'S
HOME

And when it was sunny
She'd drink tea and honey
With her friends the hare
The squirrel and the bear,
They'd eat tiny berries
And apples and cherries.

With old people she'd often find
She'd gain such peace of mind,
They'd hold her so gently
Reminiscing sentimentally
Of places and friends left behind.

And with children she'd have such fun
In their tennis shoes they'd often run,
Then they’d stop for a rest
And be Mom’s favorite guests
Then play hide-and-go-seek in the sun.

This sweet calico kitten

Knows just where it's at

About kindness and caring and

All things like that.

For she takes life in stride

With her friends by her side

So remember with fondness

The Calico Cat.

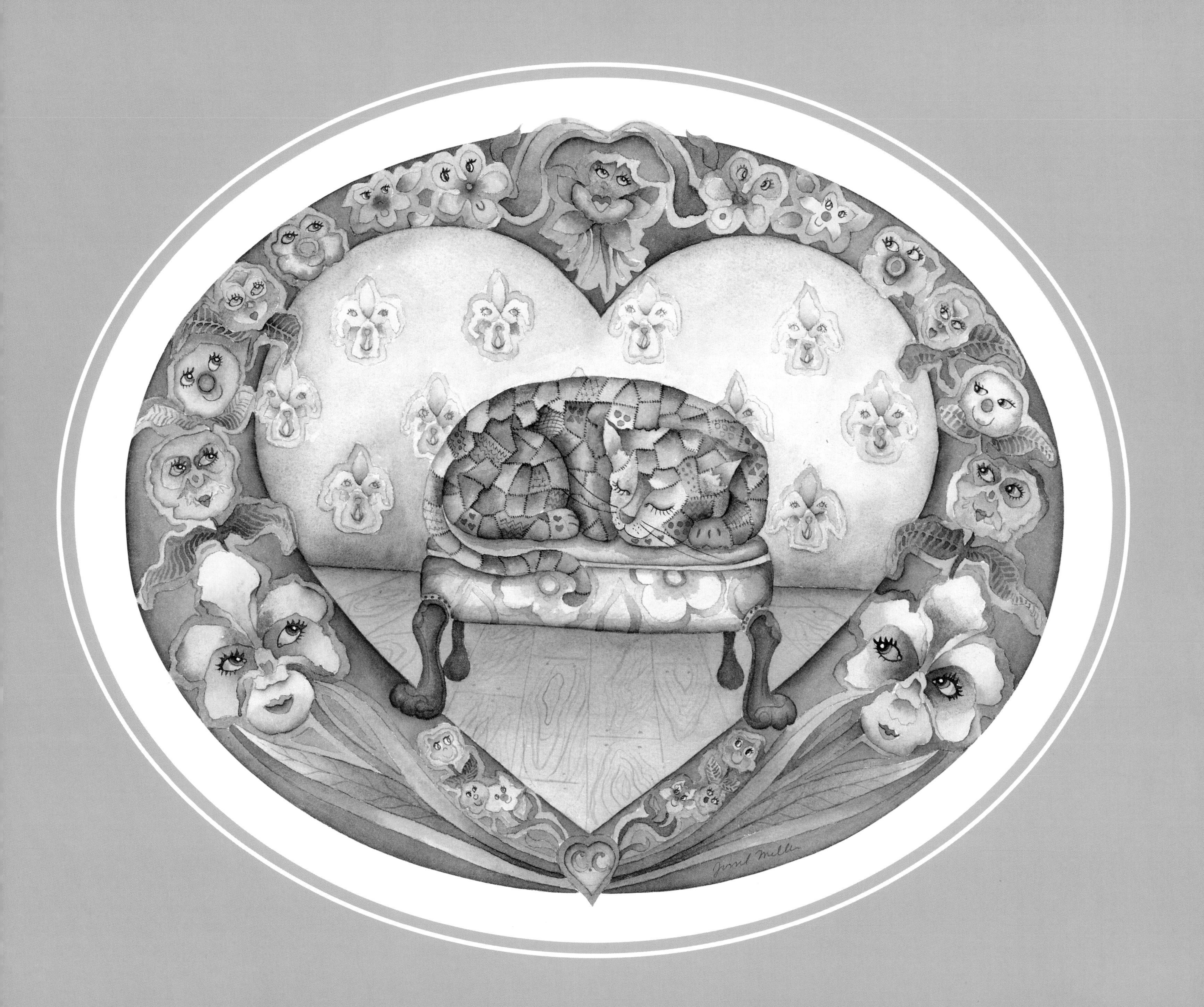

The End

As a photography artist, I strive to make magic. I create a comfortable atmosphere which allows my clients to reveal themselves.

Jessel and I have known for years that we are aligned in our creativity and playfulness. Her work and life are an inspiration to me. She is a delight to be with and I am thrilled to have the oppotunity to capture the spirit of her open, loving heart.

Rebecca Pronchick, Photographer
Portraits by Rebecca
Napa California

Photo by Rebecca Pronchick

Living their dreams, Jessel and Gary Miller enjoy life on a four acre farm complete with ducks, chickens, golden retrievers, cats, GIANT pumpkins, plus garden produce which is shared with the Napa Food Bank, family and friends.

They own and operate the Jessel Gallery and Gary's Garden Shoppe located in the heART of the beautiful Napa Valley - an oasis of creativity and voted for years, "Best Art Experience in the Valley." Fine art, flowers and gifts prevail in this serene and peaceful setting.

Jessel Gallery

Gary in the Pumpkin Patch

Jerry Alexander was born and raised in the Napa Valley and has been a professional photographer since 1986. Jerry has won numerous local awards for his images of the Napa Valley and South East Asia. His work has been featured in the *National Geographic, The Wine Spectator* and *Decanteur* magazine.

He has also done several books on Thailand and Southeast Asia. His most recent book consists of 120 images of the Napa Valley, along with a collection of twenty-two short essays by local residents, titled *Napa Valley Impressions.*

Jessel Miller

Jessel moved to Oakland, California in 1971 after graduating from the University of Florida with a degree in Fine Art and a minor in Museum Directorship and English. For many years she struggled in the art world. Graphics and fashion design were her bread and butter, yet she held her first love close to her heart and weathered great odds to make it into the fine art arena.

Her first break came in 1980 with a one person show at the San Francisco Museum of Modern Art. Jessel had focused on faces for many years and this exhibition was entitled, "Bay Area Personalities." Maya Angelou, Herb Caen, Louise Davies, Melvin Belli and Dianne Feinstein were a few of the 25 personalities she painted for a successful and entertaining watercolor portrait show.

Napa had always reminded Jessel of her small town roots of Timmins, Ontario, Canada so in 1984 she picked up her life and opened the Jessel Gallery in Napa, California. It all began with 300 square feet and 30 artists and 15 years later, the gallery is 9000 square feet exhibiting 300 artists.

Her stories reflect her childhood and her books are filled with lessons of love and kindness. Through writing and art, her dream is to carry the treasures received from her fortunate upbringing, out into the world.

She gently captures pieces of her fleeting soul that demonstrate how much alike we all really are; sparkling little jewels enlightened in the candle glowing, painted vision told in stories of the human way.

– Michael S. Bell

For more information about gifts and products from the Mustard Trilogy, order directly from:

Jessel Gallery 1019 Atlas Peak Road Napa, California 94558

888-702-6323 • voice 707-257-2396 • fax

email: jessel@napanet.net web site: www.jesselgallery.com

MUSTARD (Book One) SOFT LOVE & STRONG VALUES

MUSTARD (Book Two) JOURNEY TO LOVE

MUSTARD (Book Three) LESSONS FROM OLD SOULS

THE CALICO CAT

SELECTED PRINTS FROM EACH BOOK ARE AVAILABLE

Other Books by Jessel Miller

Trilogy

MUSTARD
A Story about Soft Love and Strong Values (Book I)

Set in the heart of the Napa Valley, this enchanting story tells of great wisdom and simple guidance to everyday living. Mustard leads the way on a crusade... to live life creatively every day, trusting in her own process as she learns LIFE LESSONS from her devoted parents and special teachers. Garden Angel - her guide, offers universal wisdom that brings order to the chaos in her life. Garden Tender teaches Mustard a balance of soft love and strong values.

MUSTARD
A Journey to Love (Book II)

This is a story about Mustard's journey to becoming a powerful, independent, self-sufficient woman - full of beauty, inner strength, and a sense of direction. Under the Mustard Moon* she meets River, a grape growing man who compliments her life with the essence of the earth and expands her understanding of soft love and strong values.

MUSTARD
Lessons from Old Souls (Book III)

Mustard and River and their children, Forest and Meadow then journey the world ~ learning new lessons from old souls. Back to the Napa Valley, they bring wisdom and to their community, teach the universal theme of LOVE. Their hearts are filled with Mustard Miracles.**

** Napa Valley Mustard Festival Poster, 1999*
*** Napa Valley Mustard Festival Poster, 2000*

The Calico Cat

Look in the mirror for a new view!